This book belongs to:

_____

For Klaus

This paperback edition published in 2011 by Andersen Press Ltd.
First published in Great Britain in 1986 by Andersen Press Ltd.
This edition with new illustrations first published in 2009 by Andersen Press Ltd. Text
and Illustration copyright © Chris Riddell, 1986 and 2009
The rights of Chris Riddell to be identified as the author and illustrator
of this work have been asserted by him in accordance with the
Copyright, Designs and Patents Act, 1988.
All rights reserved.
Colour separated in Switzerland by Photolitho AG, Zürich.
Printed and bound in Belgium.

10   9   8   7   6   5   4
British Library Cataloguing in Publication Data available.
ISBN 978 1 84270 942 9

CHRIS RIDDELL

Mr Underbed

ANDERSEN PRESS

One night, just as Jim was dozing off,

the bedsprings CREAKED ...

. . . the mattress SHOOK . . .

... and a head poked out from under Jim's bed.

"Hello!" it said. "I'm Mr Underbed."

"Hello," replied Jim. "I'm Jim."

"It's very uncomfortable sleeping on the floor under your bed every night. Do you mind if I join you?" asked Mr Underbed politely.

"Not at all," said Jim.

Mr Underbed fell asleep in no time, but his snoring
kept Jim wide awake. Jim went to the chest of drawers
to get his earmuffs . . .

... but when he opened the drawer, TWO heads popped up.

"Hello!" they said. "We're the top drawer twins, Crinkle and Crumple."

"Hello," answered Jim.

"You don't mind, do you?" asked Crinkle.

"Only it's very cramped in your drawer," explained Crumple, as they jumped into Jim's bed.

Crinkle and Crumple fell asleep
almost immediately, but they
pinched all the bedclothes
and Jim was too cold to
go to sleep.

So Jim went to the
wardrobe to get his
dressing-gown . . .

. . . but when he opened the wardrobe door, yet another head popped out.

"Hello!" it called. "I'm Weggie the wardrobe hound."
"Oh no!" said Jim.

"I suppose you want to sleep in my bed too?" said Jim.
"That's very kind of you," replied Weggie.

"I'm going to get to the bottom
of this," Jim muttered to himself.

Jim went right round his room opening
his toy trunk . . .

his cupboards . . .

his drawers . . .

looking behind
his curtains . . .

and under his chair . . . and out of all these places
more heads came popping up.

Tiny and Tubby Bear marched out of the cupboard.
Saggy and Squeak were under the chair.

Hooter the elephant and his friends, Swish and Sniffer,
peeped round the curtains.

And out came . . .

Bumble the
middle drawer
dog, Pinkie the
bedside table
rabbit, Grimble,
Grumble and Groan
the toy trunk triplets, Wid the
bottom drawer mite, and last but
not least little Willy
Glow-nose from
the lampshade.

"I give up!" said Jim.

"Everybody can sleep in my bed tonight!"

And so they did.

"Goodnight," they called

and quickly fell asleep.

Jim was quite tired after opening
all those cupboards and drawers
and so he curled up on the floor
and was soon fast asleep.

"Wake up, Jim," called his mother in the morning.
"Why are you sleeping on the floor?"

"It just seemed more comfortable than my bed last night," said Jim with a smile.

Also by
Chris Riddell

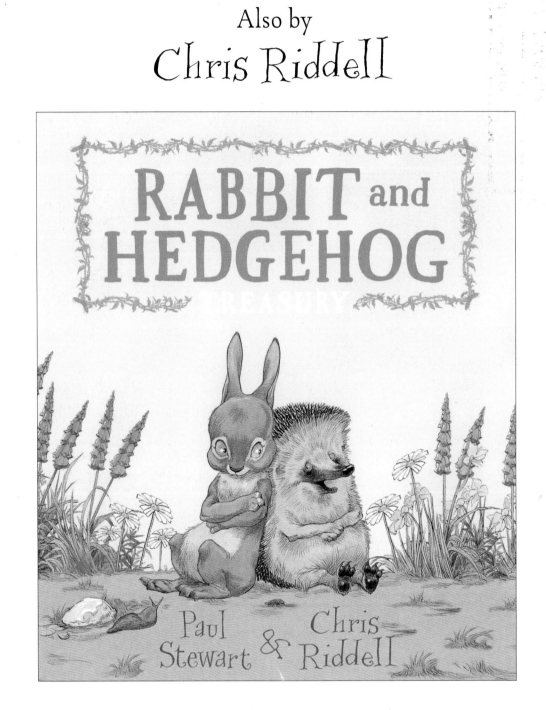

RABBIT and HEDGEHOG

TREASURY

Paul Stewart & Chris Riddell